My dear Rose,

I have so much to tell you! Despite the evil schemes of the Snake, our trip to the planet of the books had a happy ending and all the books were saved!

Our journey was as instructive as it was eventful. We witnessed again how stories can enable our spirits to travel, see new perspectives, and blossom! Most importantly, however, we learned that the most beautiful stories are the ones that spring up from our own imagination. Stories like these should never be extinguished but should be shared with others.

Fox and I are full of new stories, and we can't wait to share them with you.

The Little Prince

First American edition published in 2013 by Graphic Universe™.

Le Petit Prince™

based on the masterpiece by Antoine de Saint-Exupéry

An animated series based on the novel *Le Petit Prince* by Antoine de Saint-Exupéry
Developed for television by Matthieu Delaporte, Alexandre de la Patellière, and Bertrand Gatignol
Directed by Pierre-Alain Chartier

Graphic Universe™
A division of Lerner Publishing Group, Inc.
241 First Avenue North
Minneapolis, MN 55401 U.S.A.

Website address : www.lernerbooks.com

Library of Congress Cataloging-in-Publication Data

Bruneau, Clotilde.
[Planète du Ludokaa. English]
The Planet of Ludokaa / story by Clélia Constantine ; design and illustrations by Elyum Studio ; adapted by Clotilde Bruneau ; translated by Anne and Owen Smith. — 1st American ed.
p. cm. — (The little prince ; #12)
ISBN 978-0-7613-8762-6 (lib. bdg. : alk. paper)
ISBN 978-1-4677-1655-0 (eBook)
I. Constantine, Clélia. II. Smith, Anne Collins, translator. III. Smith, Owen (Owen M.), translator. IV. Saint- Exupéry, Antoine de, 1900-1944. Petit Prince. V. Elyum Studio. VI. Petit Prince (Television program) VII. Title.
PZ7.7.B8Pj 2013
741.5'944—dc23 2013004861

Manufactured in the United States of America
1 — DP — 7/15/13

THE NEW ADVENTURES
BASED ON THE MASTERPIECE BY ANTOINE DE SAINT-EXUPÉRY

The Little Prince

THE PLANET OF LUDOKAA

Based on the animated series and an original story by Clélia Constantine

Design: Elyum Studio
Story: Clotilde Bruneau
Artistic Direction: Didier Poli
Art: Diane Fayolle
Backgrounds: Clara Karunakara-Chardavoine
Coloring: Moonsun & Laetitia Meynier
Editing: Alcino Segusa
Editorial Consultant: Didier Convard

Translation: Anne and Owen Smith

Graphic Universe™ • Minneapolis

THE LITTLE PRINCE

The Little Prince has extraordinary gifts. His sense of wonder allows him to discover what no one else can see. The Little Prince can communicate with all the beings in the universe, even the animals and plants. His powers grow over the course of his adventures.

The Prince's uniform:
When he transforms into the uniform of a prince, he is more agile and quick. When faced with difficult situations, the Little Prince also uses a sword that lets him sketch and bring to life anything from his imagination.

His sketchbook:
When he is not in his Prince's clothing, the Little Prince carries a sketchbook. When he blows on the pages, they take wing and form objects that he'll find very useful. Like his sword, it's powered by stardust collected on his travels.

FOX

A grouch, a trickster, and, so he says, interested only in his next meal, Fox is in reality the Little Prince's best friend. As such, he is always there to give him help but also just as much to help him to grow and to learn about the world.

THE SNAKE

Even though the Little Prince still does not know exactly why, there can be no doubt that the Snake has set his mind to plunging the entire universe into darkness! And to accomplish his goal, this malicious being is ready to use any form of deception. However, the Snake never takes action himself. He prefers to bring out the wickedness in those beings he has chosen to bite, tempting them to put their own worlds in danger.

THE GLOOMIES

When people who have been "bitten" by the Snake have completely destroyed their own planets, they become Gloomies, slaves to their Snake master. The Gloomies act as a group and carry out the Snake's most vile orders so he can get the better of the Little Prince!

ARCHERS! FIRE!

AAAAH!
NOOOOO!

SAPHYRA! ARE YOU OK?

YES... I THINK SO!

TURQUOISE! IN ORDER TO WIN THE BATTLE, WE NEED TO DESTROY THEIR AMMUNITION DEPOT. BUT IT'S TOO FAR AWAY-- NO ONE COULD MAKE THAT SHOT.

TELL MARIN HE CAN ORDER HIS TROOPS TO CHARGE IN ONE MINUTE!

TURQUOISE! OUR HERO!

AAAAAAAH!

ROARRRR!

BWAAAAH!!!

WE'RE NOT IN DANGER-- THAT BOY IS! WE HAVE TO DO SOMETHING!

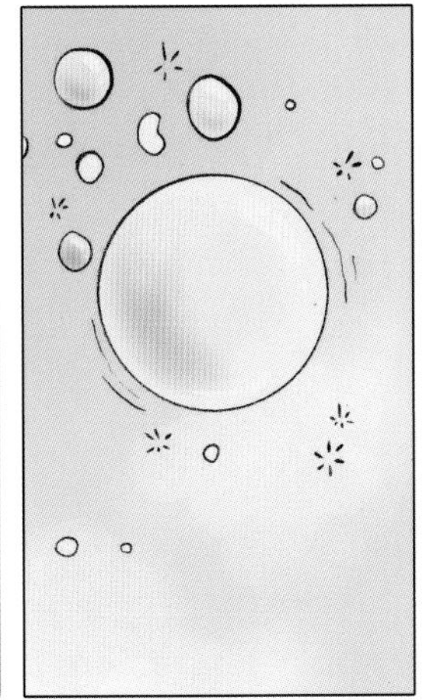

WHAT DO YOU THINK YOU'RE DOING? YOU'VE RUINED OUR MATCH!
EXCUSE ME? IT WAS ONLY A GAME?
OH, NO-- ANOTHER CRAZY PLANET!

WHAT A CATASTROPHE! STAY WHERE YOU ARE! I'M COMING DOWN!

I WAS CONFUSED! PLEASE ACCEPT MY APOLOGIES. I THOUGHT THE YOUNG MAN WAS IN DANGER, AND I TRIED TO SAVE HIM...

HA HA HA! YOU THOUGHT WE WERE FIGHTING! THE WAR WAS OVER A LONG TIME AGO.
THESE DAYS, THE AGATES AND THE AZURES PLAY LUDOKAA TO DETERMINE WHO CONTROLS THE SUNSET.

MARIN, WE HAVE TO REPLAY THE MATCH.
YES, THE SCEPTER HAS NOT YET BEEN AWARDED FOR THE NEXT CYCLE...BUT FIRST, WOULD YOU SET OUR FRIEND FREE?
THE SCEPTER?

EACH TEAM PLAYS TO WIN THE SCEPTER THAT HORIZON IS HOLDING IN HIS HAND. THE VICTORS HAVE EXCLUSIVE ACCESS TO THE SUNSET FOR THE NEXT TWO MONTHS!

I'M THE LITTLE PRINCE! I'M SORRY I INTERRUPTED YOUR MATCH. IT LOOKS LIKE FUN!
SADLY, THERE WAS A TIME WHEN WE FOUGHT A GREAT WAR FOR THIS TREASURE.

YOU LEARNED TO LISTEN TO ONE ANOTHER! SUCH WISDOM IS ITSELF A GREAT TREASURE.

TO TELL THE TRUTH, MARIN AND MY FATHER WERE THE ONES WHO NEGOTIATED THE PEACE TREATY AND DEVISED THE GAME OF LUDOKAA. I WAS TOO YOUNG TO FIGHT IN THE WAR OR EVEN HELP WITH THE NEGOTIATIONS.

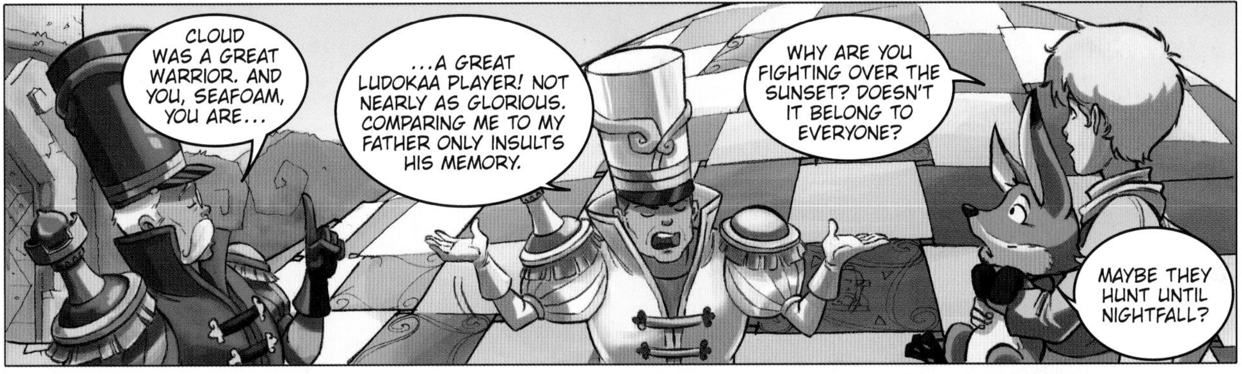
CLOUD WAS A GREAT WARRIOR. AND YOU, SEAFOAM, YOU ARE...
...A GREAT LUDOKAA PLAYER! NOT NEARLY AS GLORIOUS. COMPARING ME TO MY FATHER ONLY INSULTS HIS MEMORY.
WHY ARE YOU FIGHTING OVER THE SUNSET? DOESN'T IT BELONG TO EVERYONE?
MAYBE THEY HUNT UNTIL NIGHTFALL?

LET'S FOCUS ON THE FUTURE-- NOT THE PAST! LET'S RETURN TOMORROW AT THE USUAL TIME. BUT WE BOTH KNOW HOW THE MATCH WILL END, DON'T WE?

SO TELL ME, LITTLE PRINCE...WITH YOUR POWERS, WOULD YOU LIKE TO JOIN THE AZURE TEAM?
THAT'S NICE OF YOU, HORIZON, BUT I DON'T KNOW HOW TO PLAY! AND YOU ALREADY HAVE A FULL ROSTER.

YES, BUT WE'VE LOST SIX TIMES IN A ROW, ALL BECAUSE OF TURQUOISE...
HORIZON! LET'S GO!

YOU'D BETTER FIND A HOTEL IN THE VILLAGE! YOU WON'T BE VERY COMFORTABLE SLEEPING HERE!

I HAVE NO OBJECTION TO A COZY BED... AND A GOOD DINNER!

SINCE WAR HAS BEEN ABOLISHED HERE, I DON'T THINK THE PLANET IS IN ANY DANGER FROM THE SNAKE. COULD WE GO HOME NOW?
NOT JUST YET. THINGS ARE MORE COMPLICATED THAN THEY APPEAR, AND I'M STILL VERY WORRIED ABOUT THIS PLANET.

WHOA! THE PLAYING FIELD JUST SHRANK!
ACTUALLY, FOX, I THINK THE ENTIRE PLANET IS ONE GIANT PLAYING FIELD! THAT'S JUST ONE GAME BOARD.

LOOK, FOX! THIS MUST BE THE AZURE VILLAGE--IT'S ALL BLUE!
IT LOOKS FAR AWAY--BUT IT'S NOT--IT'S JUST SMALLER THAN I EXPECTED!

READY TO CHANGE SIZE, FOX?

LET'S FIND HORIZON. HE LIKES TO TALK--MAYBE WE CAN LEARN MORE ABOUT THIS PLANET FROM HIM!
LIKE WHICH RESTAURANT SERVES THE BEST FOOD!

I WONDER IF THEY HAVE BLUE CHICKENS HERE...YOU DON'T THINK THEY'LL MAKE ME WIN A GAME BEFORE I CAN EAT, DO YOU?

THAT'S ENOUGH, TURQUOISE! YOU HAVE TO TRAIN HARDER THAN THAT!
THAT'S HORIZON'S VOICE...

I'M TIRED OF LOSING ALL THE TIME!
IT'S NOT THAT COMPLICATED! JUST DON'T STEP ON THE WHITE SQUARES!
BUT...I'M DOING THE BEST I CAN!
STOP PICKING ON HER! SHE DOESN'T DO IT ON PURPOSE!

YOU'VE GOT A SHORT MEMORY! WHO SAVED THE DAY DURING THE GREAT WAR? YOU WERE HAPPY TO CHEER FOR HER THEN, WEREN'T YOU?
SAPHYRA, I...
THAT'S ENOUGH, SAPHYRA! THIS IS NO TIME TO ARGUE!
TURQUOISE IS TRYING AS HARD AS SHE CAN. THE REST OF YOU, DON'T FORGET THAT PEACE HANGS BY A THREAD ON THIS PLANET. IF WE START FIGHTING AMONG OURSELVES, IT'S OVER. GO AND REST. WE'VE GOT A MATCH TOMORROW!

FOX, I THINK WE SHOULD GO FOR A WALK...

WOULDN'T YOU RATHER HAVE DINNER? I WARN YOU, I ABSOLUTELY REFUSE TO MISS A MEAL!
I THINK TURQUOISE NEEDS A FRIEND NOW... AND SOMETHING TELLS ME THAT SHE COULD BE PART OF THE SNAKE'S PLANS...

TURQUOISE?
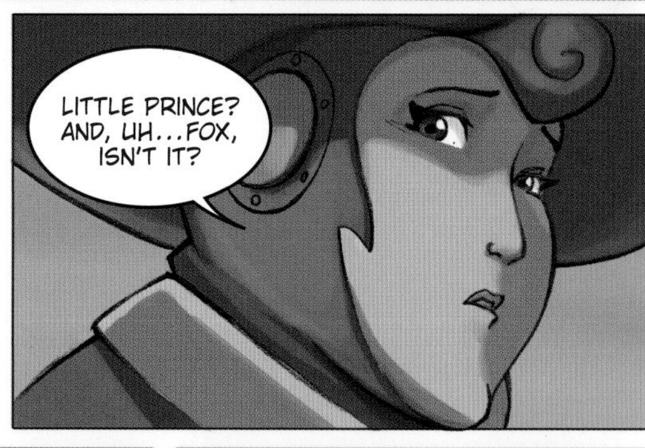
LITTLE PRINCE? AND, UH...FOX, ISN'T IT?

YOU'RE AN AMAZING ARCHER, TURQUOISE! WHAT A GREAT SHOT!
THANK YOU! I'VE ALWAYS BEEN PROUD OF MY ARCHERY. SADLY, I'M ABSOLUTELY HOPELESS AT LUDOKAA!

WHEN I PRACTICE ARCHERY, ALL MY PROBLEMS SEEM TO DISAPPEAR.

WITH MORE PRACTICE, I'M SURE YOU'D GET BETTER AT LUDOKAA.
I'VE TRIED, BUT I JUST CAN'T GET THE HANG OF IT. I PREFER TARGET PRACTICE--IT CHEERS ME UP.

SHE'D BE GREAT AT HUNTING CHICKENS!

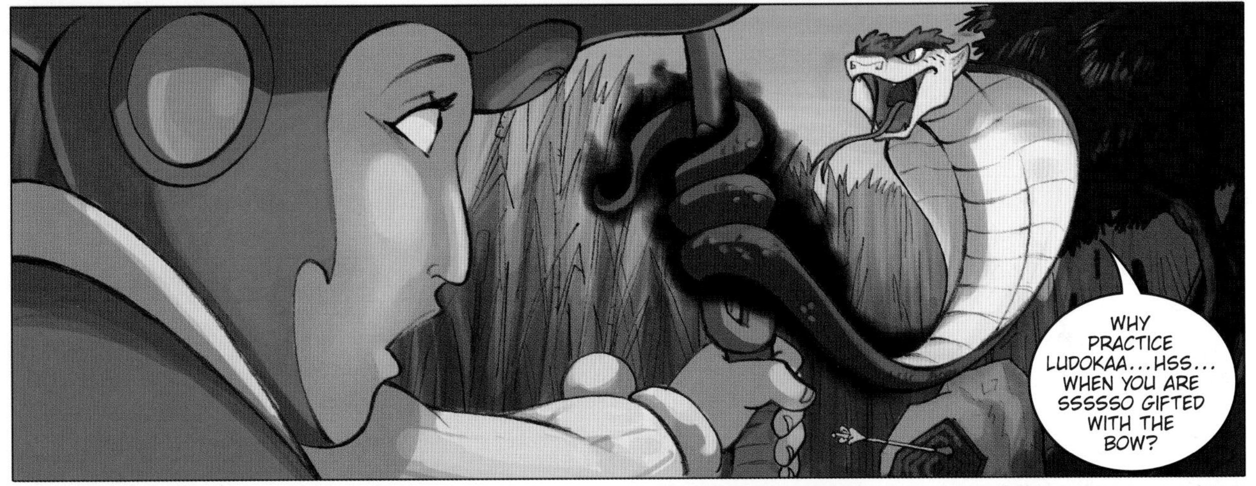
WHY PRACTICE LUDOKAA...HSS... WHEN YOU ARE SSSSSO GIFTED WITH THE BOW?

DON'T LISTEN TO HIM! THE SNAKE IS AN EVIL BEING!

I ONLY WANT WHAT'S BESSST FOR YOU, TURQUOISE. IF ANOTHER WAR COMES, EVERYONE WILL CHEER FOR YOU ONCE AGAIN... HSS...YOUR PLANET CAN'T AVOID WAR FOREVER!

NO, DON'T...

WAR? I'D NEVER PUT MY PEOPLE IN DANGER JUST TO MAKE MYSELF FEEL BETTER!

GO BACK WHERE YOU CAME FROM, YOU MONSTER! I'M NOT INTERESTED IN YOUR POISON!
TURQUOISE!

SAPHYRA? WHAT ARE YOU DOING HERE?

I WAS WORRIED ABOUT YOU...BUT WHEN I GOT HERE, YOU WERE SPEAKING WITH THAT... THING. I'M SORRY, BUT I COULDN'T HELP OVERHEARING.

THAT CREEPY SNAKE WASN'T WRONG ABOUT EVERYTHING. IF WAR BROKE OUT AGAIN, YOU ***WOULD*** RECAPTURE YOUR GLORY!

SAPHYRA! HOW CAN YOU SAY SUCH A THING!
BUT...

SAPHYRA, NO MATTER HOW MUCH GLORY A PERSON EARNS IN BATTLE, PROTECTING THE PEACE IS EVEN MORE WORTHWHILE.

THAT'S WHY MARIN AND I HAVE DONE ALL THIS...

I COULD NEVER BEAR TO PUT YOU IN DANGER AGAIN.

I'M SORRY...

PERHAPS WE SHOULD GO BACK. YOU HAVE AN IMPORTANT MATCH TOMORROW!

GO ON AHEAD--I'LL CATCH UP IN A MOMENT.

HSS...

GOOD MORNING! HASN'T THE MATCH STARTED YET?
WERE YOU WAITING FOR US? HOW KIND, BUT YOU SHOULDN'T DELAY ON OUR ACCOUNT!

WE HAVE A MORE SERIOUS PROBLEM! THE AGATES HAVEN'T ARRIVED YET. IT'S NOT LIKE THEM AT ALL!
THEY CAN'T HAVE LOST THEIR NERVE--THEY'VE CRUSHED US SIX TIMES IN A ROW!

MARIN! RETURN IT AT ONCE!

HOW UNSPORTSMANLIKE CAN YOU GET? I NEVER WOULD HAVE EXPECTED THIS FROM YOU!
WHAT ARE YOU TALKING ABOUT?

YOU KNOW EXACTLY WHAT I MEAN--YOU STOLE OUR TIGER!

IT'S OBVIOUS THAT SOME OF YOU WOULD LIKE TO SEE THE MATCH CANCELED... WOULDN'T YOU, TURQUOISE?

WHAT? YOU'RE ACCUSING ME? BUT I WOULD NEVER...

THAT'S ENOUGH, SEAFOAM! NONE OF MY PEOPLE WOULD COMMIT SUCH A VILE ACT! WE'RE NO COWARDS!

IF YOU DO NOT RETURN THE TIGER BEFORE NIGHTFALL...
THERE WILL BE WAR!

WAIT... WHAT?

I WOULD NEVER DO SUCH A HORRIBLE THING!
DON'T WORRY. NO ONE THINKS YOU'RE GUILTY.

WE'LL NEED FORTIFICATIONS RIGHT AWAY! BUILD TOWERS AS FAST AS YOU CAN!

SNOW, ORGANIZE THE WEAPONS TRANSPORT!

FIND ME... HUH? WHO ARE YOU?
I APPROVE, SSSEAFOAM... IT WAS WISE OF YOU TO SEIZE COMMAND AND ISSUE AN ULTIMATUM!

BUT AREN'T YOU THE LEAST AFRAID YOU WON'T BE OBEYED? AFTER ALL, YOU'VE NEVER SERVED DURING WARTIME, HAVE YOU?

NO, BUT EVERYONE SAYS I'M AN EXCELLENT TEAM CAPTAIN...I'M SURE NO ONE DOUBTS MY CREDENTIALS. EVEN IF...

EVEN IF A LUDOKAA MATCH IS A FAR CRY FROM A REAL BATTLE... ISN'T IT?

I COULDN'T FIGHT IN THE WAR--I WAS TOO YOUNG!

WELL, THAT'S TRUE. BUT IT WON'T STOP EVERYONE FROM QUESTIONING YOUR ABILITIES, ESPECIALLY WHEN THE OPPOSING GENERAL IS MARIN.

NOW, ***HE*** UNDERSTANDS WAR! MARIN'S PROVEN HIS WORTH COUNTLESS TIMES! HSS...

DON'T WAIT UNTIL NIGHTFALL-- DECLARE WAR NOW! PROVE THAT YOU'RE NOT AFRAID OF MARIN!

AFTER ALL, YOU'RE NOT AFRAID OF HIM... ARE YOU?

LAVENDER, HAVE YOU FINISHED CUTTING THE LOGS? WE NEED THEM BEFORE NIGHTFALL!

ANSWER ME! BAH... HEY, WHAT'S WRONG?

PREPARE TO BECOME PAWNS!
WAIT...YOU CAN'T! NIGHT HASN'T FALLEN YET!

LAVENDER! NOOOO...

YOU MISSED ONE! KEEP FIRING!

AAAAH!

HE GOT AWAY, SEAFOAM...

HE MIGHT WARN THE AZURES...
LET HIM! I KNOW HOW THEY'LL REACT TO OUR DECLARATION OF WAR. I'VE ALREADY MADE PREPARATIONS.

WHAT IS THIS PLACE, MAMA?
IT'S FORT BARIDAAL-- WE'LL BE SAFE HERE!

HORIZON! CHECK ON THE AMMUNITION SUPPLY FOR THE CANNONS ON THE SOUTH WALL!
IT'S IMPERATIVE THEY HOLD ON UNTIL NIGHTFALL!

WE HAVE TO FIND THAT TIGER BEFORE THE SITUATION GETS EVEN WORSE!
JUST HOW DO YOU PLAN TO DO THAT? CONJURE HIM OUT OF THIN AIR? WE DON'T KNOW WHO STOLE HIM!

WHATEVER WE DO, WE'D BETTER HURRY...

AND I KNOW WHO MIGHT BE ABLE TO HELP US.

WHO? SAPHYRA?

IF YOU DON'T STRING YOUR BOW PROPERLY, YOUR ARROW WON'T REACH ITS MARK...

SAPHYRA! TURQUOISE!
LITTLE PRINCE, CAN YOU HELP SAPHYRA STRING HER BOW? I HAVE TO GET BACK TO MARIN.

DO YOU THINK THEY'D LET ME FIRE A CANNON?
UH...NO! WE'RE GOING TO HAVE TO FIGHT! FORTUNATELY, TURQUOISE IS ON OUR SIDE!
ANY SIGN OF THE MISSING TIGER? I'D LIKE TO AVOID WAR IF AT ALL POSSIBLE.

AFTER YOUR LONG STRUGGLE TO ACHIEVE PEACE, IT WOULD BE A SHAME FOR WAR TO ENGULF YOUR PLANET AGAIN!

GIVEN HER REACTION TO THE SNAKE, TURQUOISE IS THE LAST PERSON WHO WOULD WANT WAR. NO, THE PERSON WHO STOLE THE TIGER EITHER WANTS WAR BADLY-- OR LOVES TURQUOISE DEARLY.

YES...I SUPPOSE SO.

AND THIS PERSON...IT'S YOU, ISN'T IT, SAPHYRA?

HOW DARE YOU? I...NO, IT ISN'T ME! YOU HAVE NO PROOF!
DON'T WORRY, SAPHYRA, I WON'T TELL ANYONE. I JUST WANT TO HELP YOU. TRUST ME.

TOGETHER, WE CAN FIND A SOLUTION. THE SNAKE'S BEHIND ALL THIS, ISN'T HE?

WHAT DO YOU SUGGEST, LITTLE PRINCE?

EVEN THOUGH YOU STOLE THE TIGER, I CAN ARRANGE...
WHAT? *YOU* STOLE THE TIGER? MY OWN SISTER?

DO YOU REALIZE WHAT YOU'VE DONE, SAPHYRA? HAVE YOU LOST YOUR MIND?
BUT I...

WHY? WHY DID YOU DO IT?

I'M SORRY! SNIFF...I'LL RETURN THE TIGER... SNIFF
TURQUOISE, SHE WAS ONLY TRYING TO HELP YOU. WE CAN STILL PREVENT THE WAR.

I KNOW, SAPHYRA...I JUST CAN'T BEAR ANOTHER WAR! WE MUST INFORM MARIN!

WAIT HERE, SAPHYRA! EVERYTHING WILL BE OK!

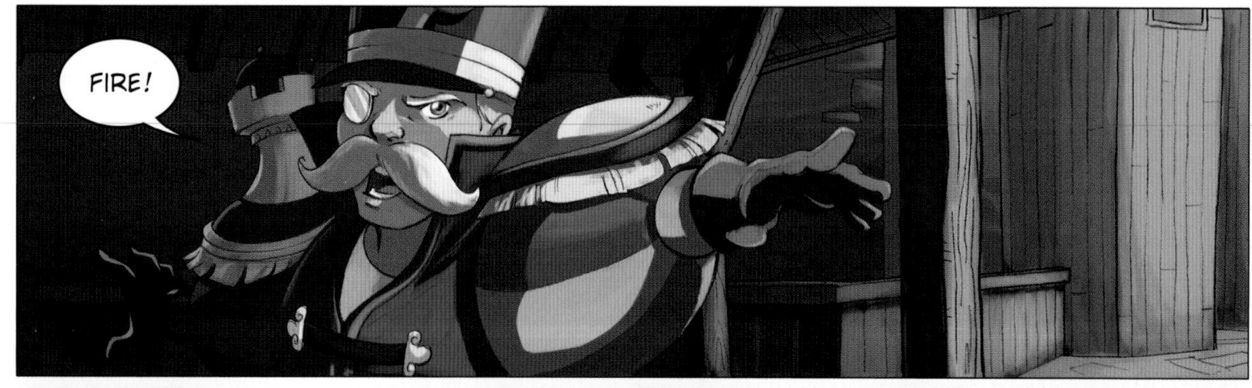
FIRE!

MARIN! THE LITTLE PRINCE HAS FOUND A WAY TO STOP THE WAR!
TURQUOISE! I'VE BEEN LOOKING FOR YOU EVERYWHERE! WHERE HAVE YOU BEEN?

WE KNOW WHO STOLE THE TIGER, BUT WE NEED YOUR HELP!
YOU MUST PROMISE TO GIVE THE THIEF A PARDON!
LOOK OUT!

TAKE COVER!

AIM THE CANNONS FARTHER SOUTH! THEIR COMMAND POST IS IN THAT SECTOR!

TURQUOISE, I NEED YOU HERE...
LITTLE PRINCE, I NEED THAT TIGER TO PREVENT FURTHER HOSTILITIES. IT'S YOUR MOVE!

YOU CAN COUNT ON ME, MARIN!

FASTER, FOX! WE'VE GOT TO STOP THIS BATTLE!
I'M GOING AS FAST AS I CAN...I DON'T WANT TO PAWN MY FUTURE!

TIME TO SCALE THE WALLS! ADVANCE!

THE ATTACK IS FALTERING! FIRE THE SIEGE GUNS!

AAAAH!

THISSS TIME *YOU* COULD BE THE HERO, SAPHYRA!
IT'S STARTING ALL OVER AGAIN!

YOU AGAIN! IT'S YOUR FAULT WE'RE IN THIS MESS. YOUR ADVICE JUST MADE THINGS WORSE!
IT'S TOO LATE TO BACK OUT NOW...HSS... THE BATTLE'S ALREADY BEGUN...

YOU MIGHT AS WELL TAKE ADVANTAGE OF THE SSSITUATION! THIS WAR IS JUSSST WHAT YOU NEED TO EARN YOUR SISTER'S RESPECT...

I CAN'T CONCENTRATE WITH ALL THOSE CANNONS...I'LL NEVER BE ABLE TO HIT THE TARGET!
THERE MUST BE A VANTAGE POINT FROM WHICH YOU CAN FIRE... SURELY YOU KNOW OF A PLACE...

SAFE AT LAST! I CAN'T BELIEVE WE DODGED ALL THOSE ARROWS!
I LIKE BEING A FOX--NOT A PORCUPINE!

WHAT SHOULD WE DO NOW?
WHERE DID SAPHYRA GO?

WE HAVE TO WARN TURQUOISE!

ARE YOU OUT OF YOUR MIND?

NEVER FEAR, FOX--WE'LL GET THROUGH THIS TOGETHER!

THERE SHE IS!
SHOOT YOUR ARROWS BEYOND THE ENEMY. WE MUST CUT OFF THEIR ESCAPE...

TURQUOISE! I NEED YOUR HELP RIGHT AWAY!
WHAT'S HAPPENING? WHERE IS SAPHYRA?

SHE'S GONE! WE'LL NEVER FIND THE TIGER NOW!

SHE MIGHT BE WOUNDED! OR... SHE MIGHT BE DOING SOMETHING FOOLHARDY!

STAY HERE, TURQUOISE, WE'LL GO FIND HER... CAN YOU THINK OF ANYWHERE SPECIAL WE SHOULD LOOK?
YES...I KNOW A PLACE...

I ONCE SHOWED HER A VANTAGE POINT IN THE MOUNTAINS--PERFECTLY SUITED FOR AN ARCHER TO HIT ENEMY TARGETS.

GREAT! WE'RE OFF! LET'S GO, FOX!

OH, JOY. MOUNTAIN CLIMBING. WHAT FUN.

GOOD LUCK! AND TAKE CARE; IT CAN BE VERY DANGEROUS UP THERE!

IF WE GO THROUGH THAT PASS IN THE MOUNTAINS, SAPHYRA WON'T BE ABLE TO SEE US--WE CAN APPROACH HER UNDETECTED.
THAT'S RIGHT--LET'S GO THROUGH THE DARK AND SCARY PASSAGE--THAT'S ALWAYS WORKED FOR US BEFORE!

LOOK! ALL WE HAVE TO DO IS GLIDE CAREFULLY ALONG THE MOUNTAINSIDE UNTIL...
UH, LITTLE PRINCE?

WE HAVE A SMALL PROBLEM...

THE GLOOMIES... WE MUST BE ON THE RIGHT TRACK!

AAAAHHHH!

WE'LL DUCK UNDERNEATH THEM, THEN SOAR BEYOND THEIR REACH!
UH...ISN'T THAT A BIT RISKY?

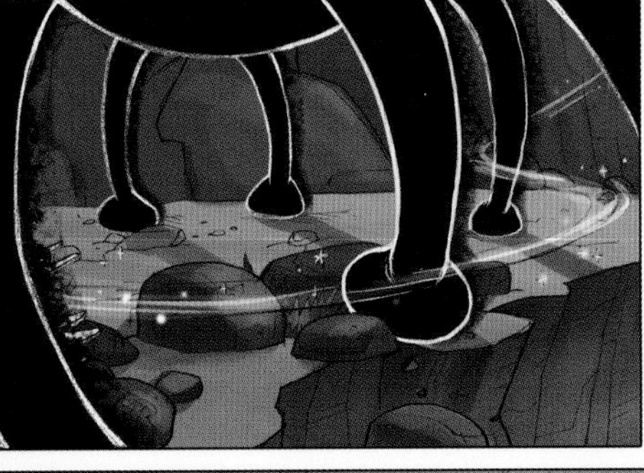

WH... WHAT? HUH?

I COULD USE A LITTLE HELP!

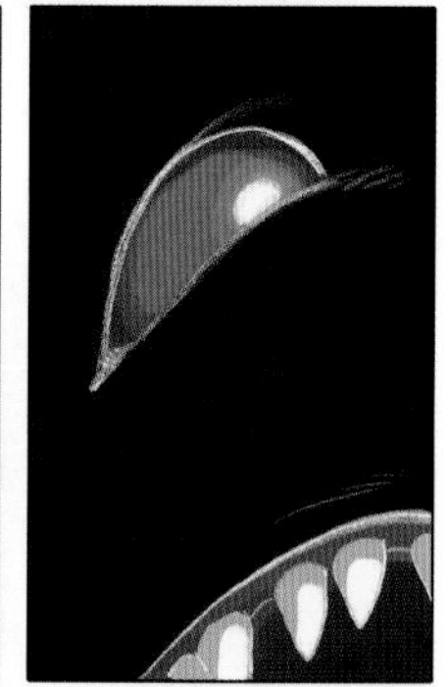

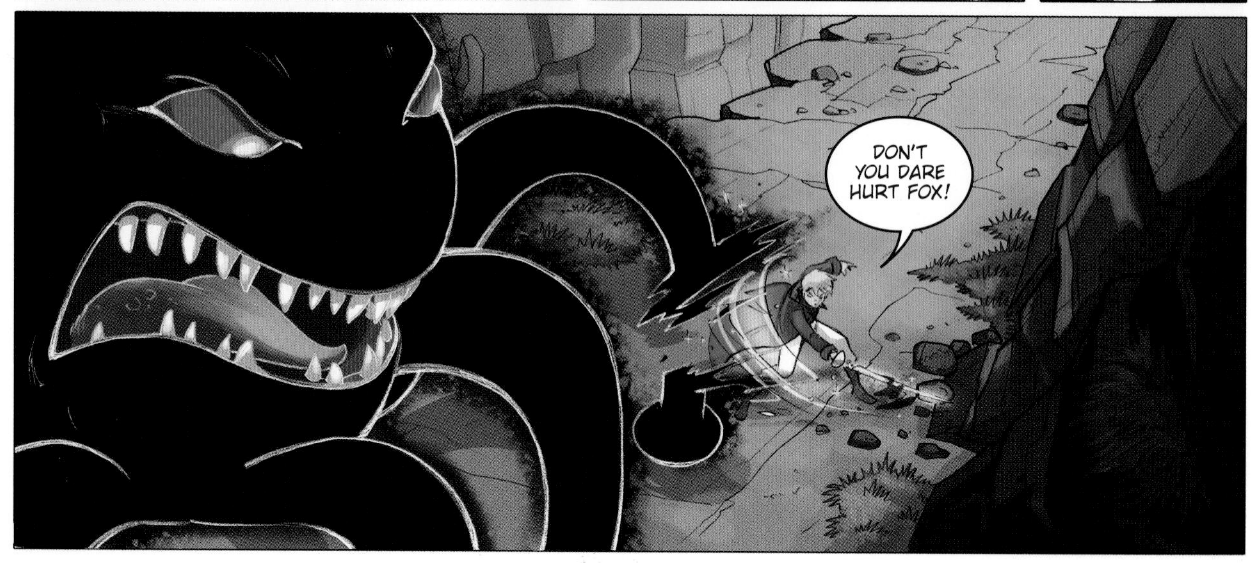
DON'T YOU DARE HURT FOX!

WHAT?

GOOD RIDDANCE!
WE HAVE TO HURRY. THE SNAKE MUST BE ON THE VERGE OF DESTROYING THIS PLANET!

LET'S GO!
HEY-- DON'T WE HAVE TIME FOR A SNACK? IT'S NOT LIKE A GIANT SPIDER JUST TRIED TO KILL US OR ANYTHING!

THERE SHE IS!

BE NICE AND QUIET, FOX!
IF WE STARTLE HER, IT'S CHECKMATE FOR SURE!

SAPHYRA! IT'S ME! THE LITTLE PRINCE! DON'T SHOOT!

WHAT ARE YOU DOING HERE? HOW DID YOU FIND ME?

YOUR SISTER SENT ME. SHE WANTS TO GO BACK TO PLAYING LUDOKAA!
MY... MY SISTER?

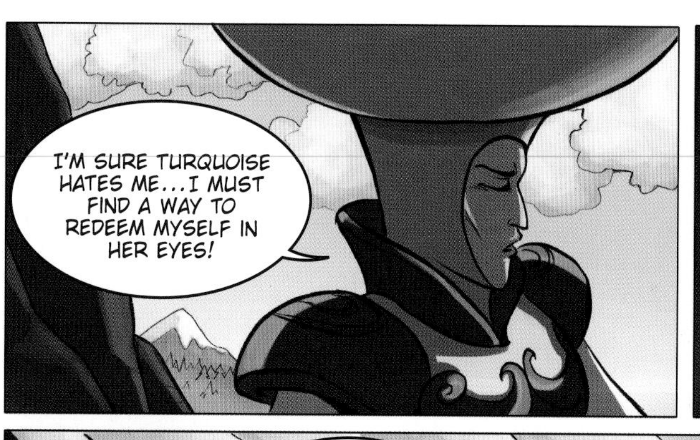
I'M SURE TURQUOISE HATES ME...I MUST FIND A WAY TO REDEEM MYSELF IN HER EYES!

YOU'RE MISTAKEN, SAPHYRA...SHE WAS VERY WORRIED WHEN YOU DISAPPEARED FROM THE FORT!

SHE'S ONLY WORRIED BECAUSE SHE THINKS I CAN'T DEFEND MYSELF...
NO! SHE'S WORRIED BECAUSE SHE LOVES YOU. UNLIKE THE SNAKE-- SHE HATES WAR AND DESTRUCTION. SHE WOULD DO ANYTHING TO RESTORE PEACE TO YOUR PEOPLE.

IF YOU BROUGHT AN END TO THIS WAR, SHE WOULD BE PROUDER OF YOU THAN IF YOU WERE THE FINEST ARCHER ON THE PLANET.

I... I DON'T KNOW.

IT'S JUST THAT...I'VE ALWAYS BEEN IN HER SHADOW, AND SHE LOOKS DOWN ON ME.

ON THE CONTRARY, SHE'S VERY PROUD OF YOU...SHE ENVIES YOUR SKILL AT LUDOKAA AND WANTS TO BE MORE LIKE YOU!

I'M NOT WORTHY TO BE HER SISTER--SHE'LL NEVER FORGIVE ME!
THE BEST WAY TO EARN FORGIVENESS IS TO RESTORE PEACE TO THE PLANET!

DO YOU THINK SO?

I'M SURE OF IT! BUT TIME IS SHORT--LET'S GO FIND THAT TIGER!
WE'LL BE THE CAT'S MEOW...HA HA HA!

I'M AFRAID WE'RE ALREADY TOO LATE!
COURAGE, SAPHYRA!

WE'LL GET THERE IN TIME!

SNOW...

WHAT HAVE I DONE? SO MUCH DESTRUCTION...

SNOW... I'M SORRY!

BUT...

IT'S OUR TIGER!

THEY FOUND HIM!

CEASE FIRE!

I ONLY HOPE WE CAN RESTORE THE PEACE...

MARIN! WHAT'S GOING ON?

THE LITTLE PRINCE AND SAPHYRA HAVE JUST ARRIVED... WITH THE TIGER!

SAPHYRA? IS SHE OK? WAS SHE WOUNDED?

I ONLY GLIMPSED HER FOR A MOMENT, BUT SHE SEEMED FINE. YOU MUST HAVE BEEN VERY WORRIED.
SHE'S ALL THE FAMILY I HAVE. I COULDN'T BEAR TO LOSE HER.

GO TO HER, TURQUOISE. SHE NEEDS TO HEAR YOU SAY THAT.

YES...

THANK YOU...FOR EVERYTHING!

SEAFOAM, IT'S TIME TO STOP THE HOSTILITIES.
IT'S TIME TO STOP THIS POINTLESS CONFLICT.
WE ALL NEED TO RELAX. LET'S EAT!

I STOLE THE TIGER. I SHOULD BEAR THE CONSEQUENCES, NOT MY PEOPLE!

THERE'S NO EXCUSE FOR MY ACTIONS.

I COULD NEVER MEASURE UP TO MY SISTER AND HER ACHIEVEMENTS. IT MAY SEEM SILLY, BUT I WAS READY TO DO ANYTHING TO PROVE MY WORTH.

SO ***THAT'S*** WHY YOU STOLE OUR TIGER?!

DON'T JUDGE SAPHYRA TOO HARSHLY. AN EVIL BEING TOOK ADVANTAGE OF HER LOVE FOR HER SISTER AND HER OWN SELF-DOUBTS TO PROVOKE A WAR ON THIS PLANET.

YOU'RE FAMILIAR WITH THIS BEING TOO, SEAFOAM, AREN'T YOU?

WH--WHAT?

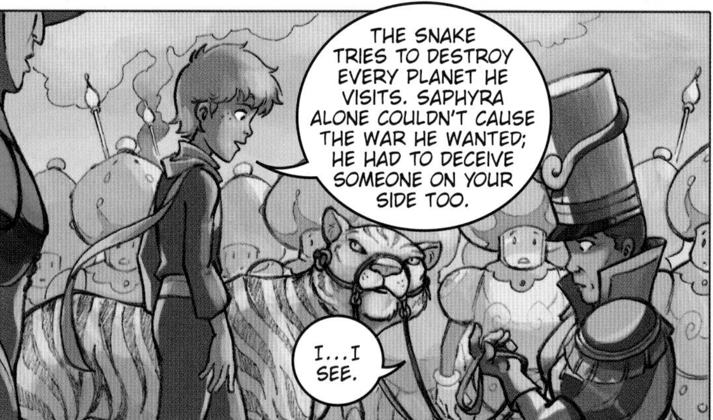
THE SNAKE TRIES TO DESTROY EVERY PLANET HE VISITS. SAPHYRA ALONE COULDN'T CAUSE THE WAR HE WANTED; HE HAD TO DECEIVE SOMEONE ON YOUR SIDE TOO.
I...I SEE.

I'M AS GUILTY AS SAPHYRA. LIKE HER, I FELT I DIDN'T MEASURE UP TO SOMEONE... MY FATHER.

TOGETHER, WE CAN RESTORE PEACE TO OUR WORLD!
LET'S NOT COMPARE OURSELVES TO OTHERS. AFTER ALL, WE HAVE OUR **OWN** SKILLS-- ESPECIALLY AT LUDOKAA!
SAPHYRA!

TURQUOISE... FORGIVE ME...
OF COURSE! I'M JUST GLAD YOU'RE ALL RIGHT.

IT'S TIME TO RETURN OUR CASUALTIES TO THEIR TRUE FORM!

READY, MARIN?
I'VE BEEN PREPARING FOR THIS SUNSET FOR MONTHS!
FOR **MONTHS?** YOU'VE REALLY GOT A PROBLEM WITH YOUR SUN!

IT'S NOT AN ORDINARY SUNSET, FOX... IT'S OUR GREATEST TREASURE!

WOW! IT'S MAGNIFICENT!

THE SUN IS SETTING INTO THE SEA OF JADE!

I WILL KEEP THIS SIGHT IN MY HEART FOREVER!

SEAFOAM? WHERE AM I? THE CANNONS!

THE WAR IS OVER, SNOW. ALL THAT MADNESS HAS ENDED!

IT'S SO LOVELY HERE-- I WISH WE COULD STAY AWHILE.

SUCH A MAGICAL EVENT SHOULDN'T BELONG TO ONE SIDE OR THE OTHER...DON'T YOU THINK IT'S TIME TO SHARE IT?

HE'S RIGHT! THE SETTING SUN IS A SYMBOL OF PEACE. IT CAN'T BE THE TROPHY IN A SILLY GAME.

EVERYONE SHOULD ENJOY IT FREELY. SO LET'S PLAY LUDOKAA JUST FOR FUN!

THIS SUNSET REMINDS ME OF MY ROSE...IT'S ALMOST AS BEAUTIFUL AS SHE IS!
DON'T BE SILLY. SUNSETS DON'T HAVE A FRAGRANCE!

THE END

Book 1: The Planet of Wind

Book 2: The Planet of the Firebird

Book 3: The Planet of Music

Book 4: The Planet of Jade

Book 5: The Star Snatcher`s Planet

Book 6: The Planet of the Night Globes

Book 7: The Planet of the Overhearers

Book 8: The Planet of the Tortoise Driver

Book 9 : The Planet of the Giant

Book 10 : The Planet of Trainiacs

Book 11 : The Planet of Libris

Book 12 : The Planet of Ludokaa